Lightning Lucy
Storms Ahead

Jeremy Strong
Illustrated by Toni Goffe

A & C Black · London

The Crackers Series

Big Iggy	Kaye Umansky
Calamity Kate	Terry Deary
The Custard Kid	Terry Deary
Eating Ice Cream with a Werewolf	Phyllis Green
Fatbag	Jeremy Strong
Fox on the Roof	Jeremy Strong
Hoods and Heroes	Nick Warburton
Karate Princess	Jeremy Strong
The Lambton Worm	Terry Deary
Lightning Lucy	Jeremy Strong
Lightning Lucy Storms Ahead	Jeremy Strong
Lightning Lucy Strikes Again	Jeremy Strong
Money Doesn't Grow on Trees	Jeremy Strong
Starbiker	Jeremy Strong
The Terrible Trials of Mattie McCrum	Janey Preger
Trouble with Animals	Jeremy Strong
Windmill of Nowhere	Terry Deary
The Wishing Well Ghost	Terry Deary
The Woff	Jeremy Strong

930381

First published 1987 by A & C Black (Publishers) Ltd.,
35 Bedford Row, London WC1R 4JH.

British Library Cataloguing in Publication Data

Strong, Jeremy
   Lightning Lucy storms ahead.—(The Crackers series)
   I. Title   II. Goffe, Toni   III. Series
   823'.914   [J]   PZ7

ISBN 0–7136–2938–X

Filmset by August Filmsetting, Haydock, St Helens
Printed in Great Britain by R J Acford Ltd., Chichester

The Witch's Cat

Lucy King sat at her desk in class and stared at the page of maths in front of her. She stared so hard that the numbers started to wiggle and change. She shut her eyes tight.

'Don't go to sleep, Lucy,' said Mr Barber from the front of the class. 'You've only been in school half an hour. Bedtime isn't for another ten hours.'

Lucy glanced up at her teacher, red with embarrassment. She nudged Paula beside her. 'How do you do number four?'

'It's easy,' her friend hissed back, which wasn't much help.

'It's only easy if you know how to do it,' Lucy pointed out. 'If you don't know then it's very difficult. So how do you do it?'

Paula put down her pencil. 'If I show you how to do this, promise you'll give me a ride after school?'

Lucy nodded.

'Right then,' said Paula. 'This number is bigger than that so it goes there. Take that away from that because you don't need it. That leaves you with 573, now add on from over there and divide the remainder and add it on to your first bit and there you are – *that's* the answer. See, it's easy.'

'I feel giddy,' murmured Lucy, as Paula pushed her book back.

'Don't forget that ride after school,' Paula went on. 'Then you can come and see our kittens if you want.'

'Kittens! Has your cat had kittens?'

'She's had five. There's a tiny tabby one and two black and ginger ones, only one has got this silly white tip on his . . .'

'Paula Lewis and Lucy King! Stop gabbling and get on with your maths,' shouted Mr Barber.

The two girls bent over their work. They had to wait until playtime before Paula could finish her catalogue of kittens. Then they had to wait until after school before they had a chance to actually see them. Lucy asked if her young brother Nicholas could come too.

'Don't forget you said I could have a ride,' Paula said. 'As soon as we get to my garden.'

'Why are you giving her a ride?' Nicholas asked. 'Mum said you mustn't give anybody rides. She doesn't like you showing off.'

'Never you mind,' said Lucy. 'Just be quiet.'

'But why are you giving her a ride? You don't give me rides.'

'I do – lots of times. Just be quiet will you? Paula helped me with some maths and I said I'd give her a ride in return.'

Nicholas walked on, thinking hard. 'All right, then give me a ride too and I'll help you with your maths.'

Lucy just laughed and called him an idiot. Nicholas pulled a dark scowl and stamped on ahead. Sometimes his sister could be a real pain, even if she did have amazing powers.

The trouble was that Lucy King was rather special. Strange things had happened to her. When she was only a few months old her pram had been struck by lightning. Instead of being harmed, baby Lucy seemed to enjoy it. Her whole pram glowed and crackled with electricity. Her parents thought it was a miracle that she had escaped and eventually forgot all about it, until a few years later, when Lucy fell into a garden pond. Before her parents could rush to save her, Lucy zoomed out of the pond and up into a tree. She could fly! Over the next few years they discovered that not only could Lucy fly, but she could make objects float around. Just lately she had developed a rather weird power of making things burst into flames.

Of course, Lucy started using her powers. She stopped a runaway coach from crashing. She rounded up an entire herd of rampaging cattle in the High Street. People began to notice her zooming about, and soon she got the nickname, Lightning Lucy, because she glowed and crackled with electric power. Sometimes you could see little sparks darting from her charged-up body.

However, being famous and special had its drawbacks and Lucy's parents did not want her to get big-headed or use her powers without good cause. They certainly did not like her giving people rides by making them float round the garden, and that was exactly what Lucy was now doing with Paula. She was standing in the centre of the garden, pointing both hands at her friend. Lucy's tumbledown hair was sticking out all over, with tiny sparks dancing in it as Paula floated idly round the garden on her back, grinning madly.

Paula rolled on to her tummy and began to make swimming movements. 'Look! I can swim in the air!' she shouted. Nicholas watched jealously as Lucy lowered her hands and brought Paula into land. 'That was great! Fantastic!'

'I want to see the kittens,' complained Nicholas.

'Yes, come on, where are the kittens?' Lucy demanded, shaking the crackles out of her curls.

Paula took them into the kitchen. There was a table pushed into one corner and underneath, at the very back, was a big cardboard box with the front cut away. Curled inside was the mother cat with her five kittens, struggling all over her like half-blind mountaineers. Paula gently picked out two kittens and handed them over.

'They're beautiful,' Nicholas murmured.

'You can have one if you want,' said Paula. 'We're looking for homes for all of them.'

'We could have two!' suggested Lucy. 'We'll ask Mum and Dad. I like that black and ginger one with the white tail.'

'I like this tabby,' crooned Nicholas, holding it up and staring into it's face. 'He's got a moustache. Look.'

Reluctantly they put the kittens back because the mother was beginning to look worried. The children backed out from beneath the table and soon Lucy and Nicholas were racing home with the news.

'Paula's had kittens!' shouted Lucy. Mrs King's eyes opened wide.

'How extraordinary! Paula's had kittens? Does her mother know? I should think she'll be most surprised.'

Lucy giggled and pulled her mother's arm. 'Oh,

you know, Mum! Her cat's had kittens and they're all beautiful and ...'

'... Paula said you could have one. The answer is no,' said her mother.

Nicholas grinned. 'Paula said we could have two.'

'The answer is still no. What about poor Flop?'

'Oh please Mum. They're absolutely angelic.'

Mrs King shook her head. 'I can remember when Flop was a kitten and looked angelic. Look at him now – he's more like a stuffed fur-coat.'

Lucy and Nicholas went on and on but their mother would not give way. As soon as Mr King came in from work they started again, describing each kitten in turn.

'They sound beautiful,' said their father.

'They ARE beautiful!' Lucy shouted.

'I like kittens,' said Mr King.

'So do we!' Nicholas yelled.

Mrs King looked across at her husband. She could see which way the conversation was going. 'What about Flop? Suppose he doesn't like it?'

'Let's ask him,' said Mr King, and he got down on his stomach in front of their old cat, who was half asleep on the floor. 'Well Flop, would you like a kitten for a friend?'

Flop turned his head away, yawned, shut his eyes and went to sleep. Mr King looked up at his wife and grinned.

Mrs King groaned. 'Oh, go on then. But only one kitten, mind you,' she shouted as Lucy and Nicholas dashed to the telephone to ring Paula.

Five weeks later a new kitten came to the house. It was the tabby that Nicholas had fancied, and the whole family agreed that with a white moustache like that he would have to be called Colonel.

Colonel quickly became used to his new home and he would dash madly around, sinking teeth into one thing and claws into another. For some strange, kittenish reason, Colonel decided one day that Flop would make a good plaything. He raced up to the old cat and threw himself onto Flop's back. Flop had been fast asleep. He woke with a startled miaow, turned on the kitten, and spitting furiously, chased Colonel into the garden and straight up the big tree. There Colonel stayed, mewing sadly in the topmost branches until Mrs King noticed. She called her husband.

'He's stuck,' she pointed out. 'Now what do we do?'

'Maybe Lucy can fly up there,' suggested Mr King. But Lucy said she couldn't get in amongst all those thin branches.

'I could levitate him down. I'll just lift him out of the tree by thinking about it and float him back to earth.'

She raised her hands and pointed her fingers at Colonel. A startled expression came over his face as he felt an invisible force plucking at his tiny body. He dug his claws deep into the bark, clutching on for dear life.

'Silly thing,' said Lucy. 'He doesn't know I'm trying to help. It's no good. He won't move.'

'I could climb up there,' said Nicholas.

'What? That high?' asked Mr King. 'Are you sure it's safe?'

'Of course. I've done it lots of times.' Nicholas was already amongst the first branches. For once he felt brave and useful. It was pretty hard having an amazing sister like Lucy, so it was comforting to have a moment of glory.

'I'm coming,' he called up to the kitten. 'You stay there and we'll have you down in a jiffy.'

Higher and higher he went, with Lucy shouting encouragement and Mr and Mrs King growing more and more nervous about him falling.

'I'm all right,' Nicholas called down.

The cat was so scared by now that, as Nicholas came nearer, he scrambled even higher into the thinnest branches. The whole tree-top was waving and wobbling as Nicholas struggled to reach the kitten.

'Take care,' warned Mr King.

'I'm okay.'

Nicholas leaned out towards Colonel. Suddenly there was a sharp crack and the branch broke.

'Help!' screamed Nicholas as he plunged earth-wards, with the branch and the kitten.

Lucy had already lifted her arms, and was calmly pointing at the tumbling branch. Power surged out through her fingers and her hair glittered with sparks. The branch slowed until it was floating down gently, with Nicholas sitting astride it like a witch, an enormous grin on his face. Colonel sat up front, still clutching the bark and wondering what was going on, while the branch went round and round the garden. Nicholas had a ride after all.

'Whheeeeee!' he yelled. 'This is ace!'

Mr and Mrs King breathed sighs of relief as the witch and his cat came into land. As soon as his four paws touched solid ground, Colonel disappeared like a flash, back into the house. Lucy shook out her curls and laughed.

'I knew that kitten would mean trouble,' said Mrs King.

Nicholas and Lucy just looked at each other. Trouble? That hadn't been trouble. It had been brilliant!

2

Spot the Difference

The door of the front room was shut tight, but it did not stop strange sounds coming out. There was a low twang and throb of noise. Lucy was doing her piano practice. She had taken the front panel off the piano and was busily bashing all the wires inside. It was a wonderful noise. She listened to the bongings and clongings vibrate and die away before she set up a new clatter of pings and plonks.

The door was thrown open and Mrs King glared at her daughter. 'Is that what you call piano practice? You're meant to be playing in the Music Festival soon! I've never heard such a racket. Put that panel back at once and do your practice.' The door slammed.

Lucy gulped and quietly replaced the front of the piano. She sat on the stool and looked at her music. It was called *Ten Tin Soldiers* and it went plonk, plonk, plonk all the way through. Lucy found it almost as exciting as a wet face-flannel. That was the problem with playing the piano. When she listened to other pianists it sounded marvellous, but when she played it herself it just went plonk, plonk, plonk ... unless she took the front panel off ...

'Get on with your practice!' yelled her mother through the door. Lucy began to go over some scales. Mum was obviously in a Bad Mood. She had not been well recently and had even had some tests done at the hospital. Lucy didn't know what was wrong but she had noticed that her mother seemed unusually short-tempered lately.

If only there was some way she could use her powers to play the piano. She could fly through the air, make things float about the room, and, if she got angry, she could even make things burst into flames – like the time she had made Maureen's desk catch fire at school – but she couldn't use her power to play the piano. Plonk, plonk, plonk. Her fingers kept getting mixed up. It sounded as if the Ten Tin Soldiers were all marching in different directions, bumping into each other and crashing to the ground.

The door opened and Nicholas poked his head round.

'Oh, sorry. I thought there'd been an accident in here?'

'Accident?' echoed Lucy.

'I heard all the noise and thought something had fallen over.'

'Oh ha ha, very funny,' grunted Lucy, launching into another awful scale. Nicholas sat down and watched her for a few minutes.

'I wish I could play the piano,' he said eventually.

Lucy carried on playing, a touch faster and more elegantly.

'I can't play anything,' muttered Nicholas.

Lucy went on. 'Why don't you learn the piano?' she asked.

'It's too difficult.'

Lucy smiled to herself and played her scales even faster. Her fingers almost tripped over themselves, but not quite. 'It's not that difficult,' she said, 'once you know how.'

'I don't see how you can make two hands do different things at the same time,' said Nicholas.

Lucy swelled with pride. 'It's quite easy when you know how, if you keep practising.' The scale speeded up until at last her fingers got wedged in a knot and the whole piece fell to bits. She turned on her stool. 'Just practice – that's all it needs.'

'I'm going to learn the trumpet when I'm older,' said Nicholas. 'You only need one hand to play the trumpet.'

'You need the other to hold it up,' Lucy pointed out.

Nicholas picked up the newspaper he had brought in. 'Have you seen this?' he asked, pointing at a couple of drawings in the paper.

'What is it?'

'A competition – Spot The Difference. If we

spot all the changes in the picture we could win a cross-channel ferry trip to France.'

'Go to France? Great!' shouted Lucy, snatching the paper.

Nicholas grabbed it back. 'It says here that the winner will get tickets for a car and family of four. Only it's very difficult.'

'Let me see too,' grumbled Lucy, sitting on the settee and peering over Nicholas's shoulder. 'There's one, look. That car has got an aerial missing.' Nicholas ringed the aerial. 'What about that ship? It hasn't got a porthole and the other one has.'

'That's just a spot of ink on the paper,' declared Nicholas.

'It's a missing porthole,' claimed Lucy.

'It isn't.'

'Is!'

The door opened again, Mrs King stood there glaring at them. Nicholas quietly folded the paper and went out, while Lucy crept back to the piano and started marching the Ten Tin Soldiers once more. Her mother watched her stonily and then shut the door. Slowly the Ten Tin Soldiers went off course as Lucy dreamily thought about France.

At long last Mrs King told Lucy she could stop. 'I don't think I can listen to much more,' she said. Then she saw Lucy's face and tried to smile. 'I'm sorry Lucy. It wasn't that bad. You can do some more later. I'm just feeling off-colour today.'

Lucy slipped round her mother and went upstairs to find Nicholas and the competition.

He had already ringed seven differences. 'But I can't see any more. It's a cheat. They just say there are ten but there aren't really and then nobody wins the prize and they don't have to give away free tickets.'

'There's one,' said Lucy, ringing a missing eyebrow on a sailor's face. 'If you win this you've got to share the prize with me.'

'Don't be daft. I've got to share it with the family anyhow.'

'I don't suppose we shall win,' murmured Lucy.

Nicholas looked at his sister. 'I don't care if *you* don't win, but *I'm* going to,' he said.

Lucy pointed out the last two mistakes and then wandered downstairs, while Nicholas wrote out his name and address and put the whole thing in an envelope.

Mrs King was resting downstairs, with her feet up on a dining chair. Lucy went and sat next to her. 'Are you all right, Mum?'

'Yes. It's just that there is so much to do and I haven't the energy to do it.'

Lucy was seized with a sudden desire to help. 'What can I do?'

Mrs King eyed her daughter, trying to think of a job that was reasonably safe. She had been helped by Lucy before, and it usually ended up with Mrs King having to do twice as much work as was necessary. 'I need some shopping: potatoes, cat food and a chicken for supper.'

'Nicholas and I can get those when he posts his letter.'

'What letter?' asked their mother and Lucy told her about the competition.

'We'd be lucky to win that,' laughed Mrs King. 'There's a spare stamp in my purse you can use. Take a ten pound note for the shopping. And Lucy!' Mrs King wagged a finger. 'Don't do anything special. *Please!*'

Lucy looked at her in amazement. 'We're only going shopping,' she pointed out.

That meant anything could happen.

They posted the letter on the way down the hill but not until they had each kissed it twice to bring it good luck and crossed their fingers. Then they stood and looked at the postbox as if they expected it to jump up and run down the High Street with their ever-so-important mail.

The supermarket was crowded.

'I wish we could fly round and pluck the things we want from the shelves,' whispered Lucy. 'How many potatoes do you think we should get?'

Nicholas said that Mum usually got lots, so they picked up a ten pound bag. They added several tins of cat food, but Nicholas said it wouldn't last very long, so they got a few extra. By the time they got the chicken, Lucy could hardly carry the basket.

'Why don't you carry it for a bit?' demanded Lucy, when her arm began to feel as if it was breaking right off.

Nicholas took hold of the handle and immediately dropped the whole lot on the pavement.

'I can't carry it,' he wailed. 'Only Superman could carry that!'

They stood there and eyed the ultra-heavy basket. Neither of them intended to pick it up.

'Okay,' said Lucy at last. 'There's only one thing to do. I'll make it fly home. Come on basket, up you get. Don't just lie there like that.'

Nicholas smiled as the basket hovered into the air. Up the hill they went, while the basket floated quietly above them.

At length a police car passed them, going slowly down the hill. The driver stared at the children and the floating basket. Then the car went slowly up the hill, with the driver still gawping at them. Then the car came back a third time and stopped. A young policeman got out and eyed the hovering shopping.

'Excuse me,' he began. 'But did you know that you're being followed?'

'Followed?' asked Lucy innocently. 'What by?'

'Sounds odd Miss, but you are being followed by a shopping basket.'

'Shopping?'

'Yes. Some potatoes, lots of cat food and a frozen chicken.'

'That's our shopping!' said Nicholas proudly.

'We've just bought it,' Lucy explained.

'Oh.' The policeman didn't know what to say

19

next, so Lucy and her brother went on home, with the basket still floating above them, and the policeman slowly following in his car. The children disappeared indoors. A moment later the policeman was knocking at the door. Mrs King answered it. She guessed straightaway that it was something to do with Lucy. The policeman began a long story about flying shopping baskets and children.

'You must be new round here,' said Mrs King, and she explained all about her extraordinary daughter. 'The other policemen know her well.'

'I must admit I got a bit of a shock. I wondered what I could say back at the police station. They'd think me mad if I said I'd seen a flying basket full of cat food.'

'I have told Lucy not to use her powers in that way,' said Mrs King, a bit crossly.

The young policeman smiled. 'It did look a very heavy basket,' he pointed out sympathetically. 'Your daughter must be rather special to you, with powers like that.'

There was a tremendous noise from next door which sounded as if an entire brass band had just fallen through the roof and landed in a heap on the front room carpet. Mrs King gave a weak smile.

'Yes, I suppose she is. That noise is Lucy doing her own rather special kind of piano practice.'

The policeman stuffed his fingers in his ears and left hurriedly.

3

Slide to Disaster

'When I grow up,' said Lucy's friend Paula one day in school, 'I'm going to be a teacher. Then I shall tell people what to do all day long.'

Lucy looked at her seriously. 'I'm going to be a footballer,' she said. 'And I shall marry Robert.'

Paula gave a loud splutter that got half the class staring at her. Mr Barber, their teacher, stopped the story he was reading to them and glared silently at the girls. Paula shut her lips tight and tried to hold them in place with her teeth. Her eyes began to water.

'Robert!' she hissed. 'You can't marry Robert!'

'Why not?' Lucy demanded hotly.

'I always thought you'd marry someone like Superman.'

'Urgh,' said Lucy. 'His neck is as thick as an elephant's leg.'

Paula spluttered again and this time she got sent out of the room. Mr Barber gave Lucy a warning glance and went on with the story, but Lucy only half listened. She kept opening the crumpled message in her hand. In heavy pencil on one side was written:

To Lucy. I love you. Robert.

Lucy was wondering what to write back.

'There,' said Mr Barber, 'we'll carry on with that another day. Lucy, tell Paula to come back in now, if she's quite finished making those peculiar noises. Before you go home, here's a letter to take to your parents. It's about a fun outing for the end of the summer term,' said Mr Barber as he handed out the letters.

'Where are we going, Mr Barber?' asked Lucy.

'Ice-skating. There's a . . .'

Mr Barber's voice was drowned in an excited babble. He waited patiently until there was calm. 'As I was saying, there is a new ice-rink at Gillingham and we . . .'

'I've been there,' shouted Leroy. 'It's brill!'

'Thank you Leroy,' said Mr Barber. 'I'm sure we shall all enjoy it. Don't forget to show your parents the letter and bring back the slip with the money. We are going next week.'

The class left school in great excitement. 'I've never been ice-skating before,' said Paula. 'Have you?'

Lucy shook her head.

'I've been lots of times,' said Maureen next to them. 'I've got my own skating boots,' she added with a smirk. She put her bag over her shoulder and walked off.

'Trust Maureen to have her own skates,' muttered Paula.

But Lucy didn't mind, as long as she and Nicholas could go on the outing. Lucy found her brother and they hurried home, anxious to discover if they would be allowed to go. Nicholas tried to practise skating on the way, but it was pretty difficult when the pavement was bone dry and he was wearing trainers.

Their father was home as he had a couple of days off to look after Mrs King, who was ill. 'Great,' he said. 'I wish I could come too. Of course you can go.'

'We thought it might be too expensive,' said Lucy.

Mr King read the letter again and frowned hard. 'Yes, you're absolutely right. It's much too expensive. Sorry.'

The brightness in their eyes died away and Lucy felt a huge hole opening beneath her feet.

Mrs King called across from her armchair, 'Don't tease them like that Harold. You are rotten. You can see they believe you.'

Mr King went red and coughed. 'I'm sorry. Of course you can go. I was only pulling your leg – well, two legs really, one each.'

'Fantastic!' yelled Lucy, disappearing upstairs.

'Now where has she gone?' asked her father.

'Can't you hear? She's putting on her roller skates,' said Mrs King, as a series of crashes and thunderous bangs came from the ceiling above.

This was followed by a hesitant thud, thud, thud, as Lucy tried to come down the stairs without slipping over.

'Why doesn't she bring them down and then put them on?' asked Dad.

'I'm going to get mine,' cried Nicholas, and he rushed out before he realised that he didn't have any of his own and had always borrowed Lucy's. Even though he was two years younger he was only one shoe-size behind her and almost as tall. He ran outside to watch his sister and see if he could beg a turn off her.

For the rest of the evening the two of them went up and down the pavement until their legs ached. Lucy and Nicholas were not the only ones practising either. That end of town seemed full of children whizzing round on skates, pretending they were on the ice-rink.

Paula and Lucy sat next to each other on the coach, until Paula pointed out daringly that Robert was sitting by himself. 'Why don't you sit next to him?' she giggled.

Lucy quickly made up her mind and slid over to Robert. He glanced sideways at her and grinned. Meanwhile Paula began sending frantic signals up and down the coach until everyone knew that Robert and Lucy were sitting beside each other.

Everyone knew except Mr Barber. Somebody gave a low wolf-whistle. Mr Barber turned round.

He could sense something in the air but couldn't pin it down. He saw Lucy and Robert sharing their seat, but there was nothing wrong with that and he turned back to the front, while half the coach sniggered and pointed. Lucy got redder and redder. Robert nudged her with his elbow.

'Don't worry. They're just jealous,' he whispered. Lucy sighed and relaxed. Of course they were.

The skating rink was in a strange building made of huge curved sheets of corrugated steel and plastic. The rink was already half-full with other skaters, slipping, sliding, falling over or whizzing expertly round. The children took their shoes off and queued up to swap them for skates – all except Maureen who had already popped on her own swanky pair and was now twirling round the ice. That was the trouble with Maureen, she was always good at everything, especially showing up other people.

Lucy got a bright green pair of skates. She slipped them on easily enough, but the laces were about half a mile long, and there seemed to be a hundred holes in her boots. Mr Barber came over and helped. He tied her boots so tightly she felt as if her legs had been set in plaster.

Lucy waddled on to the ice and fell over instantly. She got up with a laugh and clung to the sides. Nicholas came and joined her.

'It's easy,' he claimed. 'Push with one foot, like on roller skates.' He set off, a bit slow and wobbly, but he didn't fall over. Lucy followed behind. Gradually she began to get the right idea and she speeded up, pushing and sliding and wobbling crazily.

'How do you stop?' she yelled after Nicholas.

'I don't know. Just keep going.' He went off round the curve, while Lucy carried straight on and hit the barrier with a thump that knocked the breath from her. When she managed to turn round she saw Robert go gliding past, skating like a dream. He's really good, thought Lucy. Then he fell over and slid ten metres on his belly.

Lucy pushed from the side and began another weird journey round the rink. Maureen overtook her, hands clasped behind her back and skating smoothly, without effort. Lucy wrinkled her nose and tried to go faster. There was a sudden whoosh as a big teenager went hissing past, slid across to his pals and stopped on the spot, his blades throwing up a shower of ice. Lucy just managed to get her balance back when another youth sliced across her path and knocked her so hard she thumped down on the ice. Lucy sat there with eyes blazing. Mr Barber came over and helped her up. 'Are you all right?'

'It's those big boys. They go too fast,' she complained. Mr Barber nodded and said she was not the first to be knocked over by them. He skated over to the laughing group and spoke to them. They grinned and shook their heads. One by one they skated away, not even bothering to listen to Mr Barber. He was left by himself. He shrugged at their rudeness and carried on round the rink, keeping an eye on things.

Paula came past and Lucy grabbed her hand. It was easier and more fun when you had somebody to hold on to, and Paula was quite good. They went round three times without falling over, until two lads came racing up behind and dived beneath the girls' arms. They fell in a tangled heap on the hard ice.

'Those boys are spoiling it for everybody,' said Paula, as she struggled to her feet. 'Let's go to the cafeteria. It's safer there.'

Most of the school were in the cafe. They had all got fed up with the big lads. Lucy wished that there was something she could do, but as yet she had no ideas at all.

They went back on the ice for one last session before home-time. Lucy's skating improved quite a lot. She fell over twice and was knocked over five times. Even Maureen was sent sprawling by one of the lads as he charged along in the wrong direction. Then Mr Barber called the children off the ice and said it was time to get the coach back to school.

Lucy collected her shoes and wandered over to the barrier to watch the skaters that were left. The big lads now had the rink to themselves. They were zooming about, twisting, turning and generally showing-off. Lucy watched angrily. She could feel her eyes blazing and knew just what power was surging inside her.

Lucy quickly glanced around to see if anyone was watching her. Paula came over. 'Are you coming?' she asked.

'Shhh!' hissed Lucy. 'I'm concentrating!' Her eyes narrowed to tiny red dots and her body crackled. Sparks began to leap from her hair and sizzle on to the ice. Paula stepped back, half frightened, half amazed. There was a strange melting smell. Lucy glowed more and more until all at once the whole ice rink melted under her fierce gaze.

Startled yells and loud splashes brought people running to the rink. There was hardly any ice left, just one or two small icebergs, cheerfully bobbing on the surface, while the boys were now slopping about in a pool of chilled water. They were soaked through and kept catching their skates in the copper cooling tubes as they tried to wade to the side.

'What's happened?' croaked the attendant. 'I don't understand it!' He hurried off to check the refrigeration plant.

Paula knew it was nothing to do with that and all down to Lightning Lucy. She watched her friend smooth back her curls and saw the last sparks fade away. Mr Barber was leaning over the barrier, staring at the giant puddle. Trying not to smile, he watched the youths crash through the water and struggle out. Then he looked at Lucy King. She winked at him.

Mr Barber put his hands on his hips and tried to be cross, but it was no use. 'Lucy King ...' he began, but could think of nothing more to say except, 'Get on that coach and let's go home before they ask too many questions.'

Lucy grinned and went and sat next to Robert for the journey home.

4

The Sound of Music

Mrs Ruddlestone was Lucy's piano teacher. She was a tall, thin lady who wore tall, thin dresses that came down to her ankles. She had very large eyes and while Lucy played, Mrs Ruddlestone would sit next to her, staring at the ceiling. Sometimes Lucy would stop and look at the ceiling too. It was a mystery to her what Mrs Ruddlestone found up there.

Mrs Ruddlestone gave a long, long sigh. 'Lucy, dear, you do understand that the Music Festival is tomorrow afternoon?'

'Yes.'

'There will be other children there and I am sure they will be playing *Ten Tin Soldiers* quite beautifully. I'm afraid you will sound rather strange if you play like you are now. You must practise – hard.' Mrs Ruddlestone pressed a thin hand to her forehead. 'Now I have a headache. I shall meet you at the Town Hall at two o'clock tomorrow.' The piano teacher stood up and her long thin dress rustled and unfolded, length after length. She stalked gently from the room. Lucy could hear her talking to Mrs King. Lucy sat on the stool and waited.

Mrs King came in, her arms folded. 'Don't you want to learn the piano?' she asked. 'Mrs Ruddlestone is most upset. She was so sure you could manage that piece for the Festival.'

'It's boring,' muttered Lucy. 'I want to make my fingers whizz up and down and make brilliant sounds, like they do at concerts and things.'

'I know you do Lucy, but you are trying to run before you can walk.'

'I can walk!' cried Lucy.

'You know what I mean. You cannot play the piano like that until you've learnt *how* to play. You start with simple things, even if they are boring. If you keep practising you will get better and then you can move on to harder, more interesting pieces.' Mrs King sighed. 'All those other children will be there tomorrow. It wouldn't be fair to spoil it for them by playing badly.'

Lucy scowled. 'They're probably so bored they've fallen asleep in their lessons. They've probably got so fed-up they've gone into a coma and can't be woken up ever!'

Mrs King began to laugh. 'Never mind, give it one more go. I'm going upstairs to sort out some clothes for hospital.'

Lucy turned back to the music but she couldn't concentrate. She kept thinking about her mother going into hospital. It was because of the pains she had been having recently. The hospital tests had shown that she would need a minor operation. Mum and Dad said it was quite straightforward, and Mum would only be in hospital for three or four days. Then she would come home and have to rest for a while. Even so, Lucy could not help thinking about it and worrying.

Mr King came home at lunch-time because it was a special occasion. 'Fancy my daughter playing in a festival!' he said as they had lunch, and he smiled encouragingly across the table. Lucy did not feel at all encouraged and she was certain, deep in her fluttering heart, that the whole afternoon was going to be a first-class disaster.

As soon as lunch was over she was sent upstairs to wash and change. She splashed a bit of water over her hands and face and then found a dress. That had already caused one argument. Lucy wanted to wear dungarees, but her mother had insisted she put on her best frilly white dress, *and* wear a bow in her hair.

'Cor!' cried Nicholas. 'You look smart! Like a princess!'

Lucy looked daggers at him and stamped downstairs.

'That looks lovely,' said Mrs King.

'It does make a difference,' agreed her father. 'I don't think I've seen you in a dress for at least a year.'

'It's horrible,' Lucy snarled.

'Let's see your hands,' said Mrs King, turning
Lucy's palms up. 'What did you wash them with –
mud? Go and wash them properly and scrub your
nails this time!' Lucy stamped back upstairs again.
This was obviously going to be the worst day in her
entire life, and she was only nine years old.

They piled into the car and drove to the Town
Hall. Already there were crowds wandering round
outside. Mothers and fathers called to their
children as they tried to sort out where they were
supposed to go. Everybody seemed worried and
serious. A long, tall figure came striding across to
the Kings.

'Ah, there you are Lucy!' said Mrs Ruddle-
stone. 'I'm glad you could come. Now, this must be
Nicholas.' She beamed down at Lucy's brother.
'What a lovely bow-tie you're wearing.'

'It's not a real one,' explained Nicholas. 'It's on elastic. Look.' He pulled the red bow-tie so it came away from his collar. There was a loud twang as the elastic snapped and Nicholas was left holding the broken tie in one hand. 'Oh,' he said softly.

Mrs King sighed. 'Never mind, I've got a safety pin to fix it. Come on, Nicholas. Let's go and find our seats.'

Mrs Ruddlestone beamed again. 'Yes, yes. You go and get your places. I'll look after Lucy.' She began to guide Lucy through the crowd until they reached a small gathering by a door. 'Now we are all here,' said Mrs Ruddlestone. 'Has everyone got their music?' The children piled through the door chattering excitedly.

'I'm doing a solo,' said a tall, fair-haired boy called Jason.

'Are you? I couldn't! You are brave,' whispered one of the girls.

'I should get a prize,' Jason added airily. 'Mrs Ruddlestone says I'm brilliant. I expect I shall go to Music School and become a famous concert pianist.' He turned to Lucy, standing there in her dazzling frilly white dress and velvet hair-ribbon. 'What are you going to do?' Jason asked. 'Will you become a concert pianist?'

'I'm going to be a footballer,' said Lucy huskily and everyone began to laugh. She coloured.

'I am!' she insisted.

Jason sniggered. 'She's mad. Come on. Let's go and see the stage. I want to see what make the grand piano is. I hope it's a good one. I've got a Steinway grand at home, but it's not full size. I'm saving up for a proper one.' Away went Jason, his fair head bobbing above the crowd.

Lucy glared after them. She wished she could get away. She felt like zooming into the air, crashing up through the domed ceiling of the Town Hall and flying away for ever, until she reached a desert island where pianos had never been heard of, and the only music was the sound of the sea rippling on to the hot, sunny beach and a warm breeze ruffling the palm trees.

'Lucy!' called Mrs Ruddlestone. 'Come and sit here with the others.'

They sat near the stage. Lucy looked out into the audience but she couldn't spot her family anywhere. Her group were called to play their piece almost at once. There were ten pianos lined up on stage. Mrs Ruddlestone turned to the audience. 'Now we are going to hear a piece called *Ten Tin Soldiers*,' she announced. 'One two, three ...'

The march began. Ten pianos were playing beautifully together. Lucy held her breath. She was doing it! She glanced down at her fingers and began to panic. There were so many of them. How could she control all those wiggly fingers at the same time? Now nine pianos were playing together

and one soldier had gone off course. His legs were
crumpling and folding. Lucy looked at her music in
despair. It was hopeless. She put her fingers down
anywhere, everywhere, hoping to hit the right note.

'Stop! Stop!' hissed Mrs Ruddlestone. The
other players had finished long ago and Lucy had
been struggling on by herself without even realis-
ing. The children got up, bowed stiffly and left the
stage while the audience clapped politely.

'You ruined it!' snarled Jason, sitting next to
Lucy. 'You ruined it for everybody. We were all
perfect. It was only you!'

Lucy hardly listened. She wasn't worried about
the others. She was concerned about her mum and
dad who had come all this way to listen to her and
she'd mucked up the whole thing. It was un-
bearable. Lucy sat, sunk in gloom, while the
Festival went on, and on.

Thirty recorder players got up and creaked and
squeaked their way through endless dreary pieces.
Children with violins that could hardly be squeezed
beneath their chins stood in long rows and scraped

away. The audience clapped half-heartedly and looked at their watches.

Lucy sat, chin in both hands, staring glumly at the floor. 'It's no wonder you want to be a foot-baller,' muttered Jason. 'It sounded as if you were playing that piano with football boots on.'

Mrs Ruddlestone made another announcement. 'A special treat,' she began. 'My star pupil, Jason Mullet, will play for you.'

Jason mounted the steps to much clapping. He bowed, with a rather smug grin on his face. Lucy sat and watched. Jason sat at the grand piano and rolled back his sleeves. He adjusted the height of the piano stool and smoothed the music. Lucy was beginning to get rather a wicked idea.

Jason stared at the ceiling just like Mrs Ruddlestone and raised both hands to start. Just as he brought down his hands the piano lid slammed shut, and he banged out the first chord on the wood. There was a gasp from the audience. Jason opened the lid carefully and checked it. He raised both hands to start again. This time, the whole piano slid away from him. His hands whooshed through the air silently and hit his knees. Lucy giggled quietly, and hoped nobody would notice her crackling away on her seat.

Mrs Ruddlestone stared hard at the piano and shook her head. It was a mystery to her. Jason pulled his stool over to the piano and warily began

to play. Lucy watched and waited. This would teach him not to make fun of her! Slowly, the piano began to slide away from the stool. Jason leaned forward, stretching out his arms to reach the retreating piano. He fell off the stool.

The audience began to buzz, wondering what was going on. Mrs Ruddlestone made some kind of excuse, while Jason glared at the piano and marched off stage. But even while this was taking place there was a gasp from the audience as Lucy went zooming into the air, trailing glittering sparks like little fireworks in her wake.

'It's Lightning Lucy! Didn't recognise her in that dress. What's she going to do?'

A moment later the excited audience found out. Down on the stage the grand piano rumbled and creaked and slowly lifted into the air, shimmering in a red glow as Lucy raised it until it hovered beneath the big domed roof. She swooped up to the

piano and began to play *Ten Tin Soldiers*, hovering in mid-air.

It was not a perfect performance. In fact there were a lot of mistakes, but the audience didn't notice. They were too busy enjoying the wonderful spectacle of the flying pianist. It certainly made the Music Festival much more exciting.

Lucy finished the piece and came back to earth with a little bump. Mr and Mrs King were waiting, not at all pleased.

'You did that to Jason, didn't you?' said her father angrily. 'It was very unkind.'

But Lucy didn't think so. Jason was so big-headed he would soon get over it, and he had been rather nasty to her. Besides, the concert was so boring until she had done her party-piece.

Nicholas came up and whispered to her. 'That was fantastic,' he said, 'but you still made too many mistakes.'

5

Time for a Shower

Mr and Mrs King soon forgot about the Music Festival. They had their minds taken up with more important matters as Mrs King prepared to go into hospital for her operation. She kept writing out long lists of what would need doing in the house while she was away. 'Don't let the washing pile up,' she said.

'I won't,' said her husband.

'And make sure the ironing gets done.'

'Stop worrying. I'll see to it. Have you got everything you need? Toothbrush? Suitcase?'

Mrs King nodded. The whole family felt on edge. After all, it was not every day that one of them went into hospital for an operation. As they got in the car Mrs King turned to Lucy with a ghost of a smile. 'Now I know how you felt when you had to play that piece of music on stage,' she said. 'I've got butterflies in my stomach.'

Mr King laughed. 'It's no wonder you're having an operation. Poor things – fancy fluttering about down in your insides.'

The hospital seemed modern from the outside, but inside it was just like any other, with a tangy smell of antiseptic and disinfectant everywhere. A nursing sister showed them to the right ward.

'This will be your bed, Mrs King. If your family would like to wait outside for a few minutes, you can get your bedclothes on and make yourself comfortable.' The nurse pulled thick curtains round Mrs King's bed and she vanished from view.

Lucy, Nicholas and Mr King waited outside, sitting uncomfortably on the edge of their seats. They sat in silence, unable to think of anything to say to each other. All their thoughts were with Mrs King. It seemed ages before the sister came to the door and invited them back into the ward. The screen had been pushed back, and Mrs King was sitting up in bed, smiling. 'I feel silly, sitting in bed in the middle of the day,' she said.

'You don't look silly,' answered her husband.

'Don't forget to buy some eggs, will you?' reminded Mrs King, still worrying about how they would manage. 'And don't forget onions either.'

Mr King bent forward and kissed his wife's cheek. 'We're not idiots,' he said. 'Stop fretting. We'll be fine.'

All too soon it was time to leave. The doctor came to examine Mrs King, and the rest of the family were told to go home and come back in the evening, when the operation was over. They kissed their mother goodbye and walked out of the ward, feeling very strange as they left her behind.

'I hope she'll be all right,' murmured Lucy.

'Of course she will. You'll see, when we come back this evening. Now, let's get home. Mum's going to be away a few days and when she gets back I want her to have a surprise.'

'What sort of surprise?'

Mr King grinned at the children. 'We are going to put a shower unit in the bathroom,' he announced. 'We're going to add extra piping to carry the hot and cold water. We shall have to tile some of the walls in the corner and put in a shower-tray. I've already bought that and hidden it in the garage. Then we connect up the shower, put in a curtain rail, a curtain and hey presto!'

'Is it really as easy as that?' asked Lucy.

'Of course it is,' said their father confidently. He had never put up tiles, or showers, nor done any plumbing before. 'It will be such a nice coming-home present for Mum.'

Mr King was also thinking that the work would help keep everyone's minds off the operation.

When they reached home Mr King showed them the shower-basin. It was made of moulded blue plastic. He pushed it into one corner of the bathroom and explained where everything had to go. First of all they had to put in the plumbing. That meant two new sections of copper tubing had to be connected to the pipes under the bath.

Mr King went downstairs and turned the mains water supply off, so they could cut holes in the pipes without drowning themselves.

He shone a torch under the bath. 'Hmmm. There are lots of pipes here,' he called out. 'But I'm sure I know which one is which. Pass me one of those special adaptor valves, Nicholas.'

Mr King began to bang and thump. He shouted 'Ow!' several times and one or two other words that shouldn't be written down. Lucy and Nicholas sat on the edge of the bath grinning at each other. Every so often they passed down some copper tubing, or more valves, and gradually two long snakes of copper pipe came out from beneath the bath and wriggled their way to the shower tray and up the wall. Mr King fixed the shower unit on the end.

'We'd better test it before I fix it to the wall properly,' he said. 'Turn the mains on downstairs.'

Lucy ran down and turned the tap back on. Water gurgled round and round the pipes, filling the tanks in the loft.

Mr King turned on the shower. Nothing happened.

'I don't understand,' he grumbled. He tried the bath taps, but only the hot tap worked and that delivered cold water. Mr King scratched his head. He pulled the lavatory chain to see if that still flushed properly. It did, but with hot water. Steam billowed from the bowl.

Lucy and Nicholas were giggling madly, while Mr King wandered round the bathroom wondering what had gone wrong.

'I'm going to call a plumber,' he snapped at last. 'Come on, it's time we went back to the hospital.' He stalked off downstairs.

'Not a word about this to your mother,' he said in the car. 'It's going to be a surprise.'

Lucy said it probably would be a surprise when Mum found hot water flushing the loo bowl.

Mrs King was sitting up in bed, waiting for them. She was propped up on four big pillows, and although she looked pale, she was wide awake and smiling.

'Are you all right?' asked Lucy.

'Can I see the cut?' demanded Nicholas immediately.

Mum started to laugh and quickly winced. 'Ouch. It hurts when I laugh. It pulls on the stitches. I'll show you when I come home and the dressing has been taken off. I haven't even seen it myself yet.'

Mr King sat on the edge of the bed and asked how the whole operation had gone. Apparently the doctor had already been round and told Mrs King that it was quite simple and successful. 'So,' went on Mrs King, 'no more awful tummy-pains or backache. And I can come home in two days if I start to heal well.'

Mr King's jaw dropped. 'Two days! That doesn't give us much time.'

'Time for what?' Mrs King was very puzzled.

'Oh, you know,' said her husband, hurriedly trying to think of something.

'He's worried about the ironing,' said Lucy, coming to her father's rescue.

'I told you not to let it pile up,' reminded Mrs King.

They left her some fruit and flowers and went home feeling much happier, now they could see that their mother was getting better and the worst was over.

'Two days doesn't give us much time to finish that shower,' said Mr King. 'We'd better get a move on.'

As soon as they opened the front door Mr King knew something was wrong. There was water pouring down the stairs for a start. He gave a yell and dashed up to the bathroom. There were more yells, a sudden crash of splintering wood and a scream. Something shattered on the kitchen floor and Lucy ran in to find water cascading down through a large hole in the ceiling. There was her father, jammed in the hole, his legs wriggling about and water pouring down around him. A muffled shout came from above. 'Help! Turn the water off, Ooof! Get me out!'

Nicholas joined in. 'Lucy, come up here, quick!'

Lucy half ran, half flew upstairs and dashed into the bathroom. Water was spraying out all over the place from the new shower unit. Lucy was instantly soaked to the skin, like the others.

'Keep back!' yelled their father. 'The floor must have been rotten and the water's made it go soggy. That's why I fell through. I'm stuck. Stop the water!'

Lucy stared at the pipe where the water was spraying out. Her eyes went red and tiny. She focused her fierce glare on the copper pipe, slowly welding over the hole until the spray stopped.

'Well done,' panted her father. 'Get a plank from the garage and lay it across the floor.'

Nicholas raced downstairs and came struggling back with a plank, which they pushed in front of their father. He rested his arms on it and gradually pulled himself clear of the hole and crawled to the bathroom door. They sat on the floor looking at the soggy mess.

'I don't think this is the kind of shower Mum would like,' said Mr King.

'I wish I'd had a camera,' said Lucy. 'You looked really funny with your legs hanging through the kitchen ceiling.'

Her father groaned. 'There isn't mess down there too, is there?'

Lucy nodded. Mr King gave another groan and went down to investigate. He squelched out of the kitchen looking very depressed. 'I shall have to phone the builder as well as the plumber. I give up. I should have got them in straightaway. This will probably turn out to be the most expensive shower in the history of bathrooms.

'Can't we do the tiling?' asked Nicholas hopefully.

'I don't think so. The way our luck is going the whole wall will fall down if we so much as lay a finger on it. I hope the builder can finish before Mum comes home.'

It was a strange house they slept in that night. It was probably the only place in the country with a hot-water lavatory, cold bath and a hole through to the room below.

'If Mum sees this I should think she'll turn round and go straight back to the hospital,' said Lucy, as she went to bed.

'I think I'll join her,' groaned her father. 'Good-night, Lucy, and thanks for your help. I didn't know you could weld metal like that.'

Lucy grinned up at her father. 'Neither did I,' she admitted. 'But there's a first time for everything, isn't there?'

'First *and* last for my plumbing,' grunted Dad.

6

The Home Help

When Mrs King came home from hospital the house was clean and tidy. The shower was in place, the hole in the floor was mended, the ironing and washing had all been done. A builder friend of Mr King had seen to the bathroom. It had cost quite a lot of money but Mr King was secretly pleased that he hadn't had to sort out the problems himself. The shower cubicle looked splendid, and it really was a surprise for Mrs King.

'My goodness! Did you do that?' was her first question.

'Well yes ...' began her husband.

'And no ...' added Nicholas, honestly.

'We did some of it,' said Lucy. 'Mostly the first bit.'

Mrs King looked from one to another, not knowing what to make of it.

'What was the first bit?' she asked.

'The most difficult bit,' said Nicholas.

'The most exciting bit,' added Lucy, grinning. Again Mrs King looked from one to another, feeling slightly confused. She did think that the shower looked very nice and said she couldn't wait to use it.

'One day we shall tell you the whole story,' said

her husband, 'but not quite yet, because we haven't recovered from it yet, have we?'

Nicholas and Lucy agreed, although Lucy was rather sad that the lavatory had been put right. She secretly wished that it still flushed hot water. The doctor came to the house and told them that Mrs King would have to rest for some time and take only a little exercise at first. No housework for a while.

'Oh good,' smiled Mrs King. The doctor didn't laugh.

'I mean it, Mrs King. You must find someone to come in and clean and cook for you. Perhaps your husband and children can help?'

'Of course we will,' said Lucy. 'We're good at helping.'

'I have a couple more days off before I have to go back to work,' said Mr King. 'We'll sort out a routine and follow that. It shouldn't be too difficult.'

Mrs King was already closing her eyes, half asleep. The doctor said she would be like that for a while. 'It's the anaesthetic wearing off. She'll be tired for two or three weeks and then get back to normal quite quickly.' She packed her case and left, while Mrs King fell fast asleep on the settee.

The rest of the family sat down and tried to work out a plan. Nicholas said he would make breakfast and tidy bedrooms. Lucy offered to sort out washing, change the beds and vacuum the carpets.

'That's fine.' agreed their father. 'I'll sit back and watch you both.'

'You can't!' yelled Lucy and Nicholas together.

'Ssssh,' said their father. 'You'll wake Mum.'

'I am awake,' she said, opening one eye. 'Dad can cook lunch and tea, do the washing-up and the drying-up, rinse the basins, feed the cats, do the ironing and . . .'

'Hold on, hold on, that's not fair,' wailed Mr King.

'Yes it is. You're twice as big as the children, so you can do twice as much. Now stop disturbing my beauty sleep.'

'I'll send you back to hospital if you go on like that,' warned Mr King.

The children started out well. Nicholas did have one or two problems with breakfast. He burnt the toast and made the tea with sugar in the teapot, but it made life more interesting. At length though they got bored with picking up bits of dirty clothing and endlessly cleaning and tidying.

Lucy was fed-up with pushing the vacuum cleaner round and round, and tried to think of a more exciting way of doing the housework.

First of all she concentrated her powers on the vacuum cleaner. She sat back in a nice comfy arm-chair while she made the cleaner wander backwards and forwards over the carpet. She called Nicholas in to watch, and as soon as he came in she made the vacuum cleaner chase him round the room, with the nozzle waving in mid-air and sucking at his pullover. He was not impressed.

'It's all right for you, but I can't do things like that.'

Lucy carried on controlling the cleaner.

'What I need,' Nicholas complained, 'is a robot to do my work. I'm worn out.'

Lucy thought a robot sounded a great idea and was so busy thinking about it that she forgot to keep her thoughts on the vacuum cleaner. Before she knew what was happening, it had swallowed the table-cloth and climbed halfway up the wall. She brought it back to the ground and switched off quickly.

It was then Lucy realised she hadn't seen Colonel for some time.

Nicholas stared at his sister in horror. 'You haven't sucked the kitten into the vacuum cleaner have you?'

Lucy bit her lip. 'I don't think so. I'm sure I would have noticed.'

Nicholas seized the machine and ripped off the lid. He tipped out the dust bag and a cloud of filth billowed into the air.

'Urgh!' coughed Lucy and at that moment she heard a little mew. There was the kitten, clutching

on to the topmost bookshelf where he had dashed to escape the roaring vacuum monster. Lucy lifted him down and took him through to a quieter room. Then they set about clearing up the mess they had just made. When that was finished Lucy said she would help her brother with the washing-up.

Lucy had a strange way of tackling it. The dirty plates were by the side of the sink and Lucy made them fly round the room, one by one, before dive-bombing into the washing-up bowl and sending showers of soap suds over the edge. After a quick dip the plates took off once more, this time with Nicholas in hot pursuit, waving a tea-towel and desperately trying to dry them.

Unfortunately Lucy got a little too clever and tried to make six plates fly in formation. The experiment got a bit out of control and three plates crash-landed in bits, while the other three wobbled dangerously on, and were only saved by Nicholas snatching them from mid-air as they passed over his head.

Mrs King came in to see what the noise was. Lucy was on her knees with the dustpan and brush, clearing up broken plates.

'What happened?' asked Mrs King.

'Three of the plates slipped,' Lucy mumbled.

Her mother wondered how and why the plates had slipped. She was pretty sure she could make a good guess. She was quite used to Lucy's awkward powers. Besides, she could still see a vague glow round Lucy's hands.

'Try and do the washing-up normally, Lucy. Then you're unlikely to break any more plates. You're supposed to be helping.'

Lucy finished off washing-up the boring way, while her mother went to lie down.

A little later Nicholas came from the hall with some post that had just been delivered. 'There's a letter for me,' he said, surprised.

'I never get any letters,' Lucy moaned.

'You never write to anybody,' Nicholas said.

'Neither do you.'

'But I've still got a letter,' said Nicholas as he opened it, pulling out a large sheet of paper. He began to read.

'What does it say?' asked Lucy, trying to peer over his shoulder.

'I don't know. I can't read half the words. They're too long.' He held it so that Lucy could see and she began to mouth the words quietly to herself, gradually getting louder as she got more excited. '. . . and your answer was picked out first from the postbag. We are therefore delighted to inform you that you have won the prize of a day-trip to France for a family of four . . . Nicholas! It's that Spot The Difference Competition! We've won it!'

'Oh wow!' breathed Nicholas, taking back the letter. 'I don't believe it. I've never been to France. Can you speak French?'

Lucy shook her head. 'Let's see when we can go.' She read through the letter again. 'It says we can take the trip at our own convenience. What does that mean?'

Nicholas didn't know, and he suggested they asked their mother. They dashed madly upstairs and burst into her room. She was half asleep but the children soon had her eyes wide open.

'How lovely,' she said. 'I've always wanted to go to France. You're very clever Nicholas.'

'I did it too,' Lucy insisted.

'Dad will be pleased. As soon as I'm recovered we'll go over to Boulogne for the day. That will be something to look forward to.'

Mrs King allowed her head to sink back against the pillow. 'I feel so tired still. Let me get a bit of sleep now. You did say you would change all the beds today before Dad got in. See if you can give him a double surprise and get that done, as well as telling him the other great news.' Mrs King smiled at them both, closed her eyes and went back to sleep as they raced off.

Changing the beds was tiring work for the children. Each bed had to be stripped down and have fresh sheets. When they reached their mother's room they realised they had a problem. She was still fast asleep.

'How can we change that one?' asked Nicholas.

'Watch.' Lucy's hair crackled faintly and she pointed her hands at her mother. Bit by bit Mrs King rose into the air, with a blanket trailing round her. She was snoring quietly.

'Quick!' whispered Lucy. 'Get those covers off and change them.'

Nicholas grabbed the covers and whipped them off. He spread a fresh sheet and tucked it in. Lucy kept her mother hovering near the ceiling until the bed was finished, then slowly brought her back down. Nicholas gave his sister a silent thumbs-up sign and they crept from the room, leaving their mother still fast asleep and none the wiser.

Only when they were safely out of earshot did they collapse into hysterical laughter and then rush outside to find something even more exciting than housework to do.

7

Food for Thought

'I can hardly believe this,' said Mr King, as they drove to Dover. 'Here we are, setting off for France with free tickets, all because Nicholas spotted ten things wrong in a competition.'

'I found some of them,' Lucy reminded everyone.

'Only another fifteen miles,' said Mrs King, glancing at a passing signpost. 'I'm getting excited. I do hope the sea's calm. The last time I went in a boat was a bit of a disaster.'

'Why? What happened?' asked Nicholas.

'It was when your dad and I were young. We went to a boating lake and . . .'

'Yes,' interrupted Mr King. 'The children don't want to hear about that.'

'Oh yes we do!' Lucy and Nicholas shouted.

'Your father hired a rowing boat and I thought he was really manly. He made me sit in the middle of the boat while he got the oars and sat up one end, but he couldn't find anywhere to put the oars . . .'

Lucy started giggling.

'Then your dad realised I was supposed to sit at the end and he had to go in the middle. So we changed places and he almost fell overboard . . .'

'No I didn't!'

'Yes you did. Anyhow, he put the oars in those horseshoe things . . .'

'Rowlocks,' snapped Mr King.

'And shoved the oars in the water. He pulled so hard he fell over backwards into the bottom of the boat. All I could see were two legs waving in mid-air.'

Nicholas laughed out loud and Lucy was about to say that it sounded like the time Dad tried to put a shower in the bathroom and fell through the floor. She stopped herself in the nick of time.

'We spent most of the afternoon going round and round in circles. Eventually he dropped one of the oars and it floated away. So he paddled after it and tried to grab it with the other oar . . . until he dropped that one too. Then we heard a voice shouting, "Come in, Number Four, your time is up!" I told Dad we had to go back and he said how could we get back without any oars?'

The two children were doubled up. Lucy had tears rolling down her cheeks, while their father angrily drove faster and faster.

'It's not that funny,' he fumed.

'It is, it is!' screamed Lucy.

'What happened?' asked Nicholas.

'They sent out another boat and towed us back,' laughed Mrs King. 'But that wasn't the end of it. I got out of the boat and when your dad tried to follow, he tripped over that horseshoe thing you put the oar . . .'

'The rowlock!' shouted Mr King again.

'. . . and fell straight into the pond!'

By this time they were laughing so much they hardly heard Mr King announce in a chilly voice that they had reached the port. He slowed down and handed over the passports for checking.

'There it is!' shouted Nicholas. 'That big white one. You can see its funnel behind the crane.' They went slowly up a long ramp and down the other side. Before they even realised, they were inside the belly of the ferry and were being shown where to stop. As they got out they could see car after car driving on to the boat behind them. Mr King locked up and they made their way to one of the big lounges. Mrs King made herself comfortable next to a low table and the family sat down. Nicholas immediately got up again.

'I'm going to explore,' he announced.

'Me too,' said Lucy, jumping to her feet.

'Don't get lost,' warned their father hopefully, as the two children ran off. He turned back to his wife. 'Peace at last.'

Lucy and Nicholas managed to explore the entire boat in about ten minutes. They went upstairs and downstairs from bow to stern, and finally settled for peering over the back to see when the great ropes that moored the ferry would be cast off.

The boat gave a blast on her siren and the dockers began uncurling the ropes. They were thrown into the sea and winches pulled them up on board.

'We're moving!' yelled Lucy, as the boat slowly rocked away from the jetty and began to gather pace. She raced back to the lounge and skidded up to her parents. 'We're moving!' she screamed, turned tail and raced back to Nicholas.

'What was that about peace?' asked Mrs King.

Almost two hours later France was sighted and the ferry pulled into Boulogne harbour. 'It looks just like England,' Nicholas complained.

'That sign isn't in English,' said his father. 'Come on. Let's go down to the car. Remember, this is France we are in. Nobody will understand our English, and Lucy . . .'

'What?'

'Please remember that nobody here knows about your special powers. Don't use them.' Lucy nodded. She was only half listening, being too busy watching the front of the ship open up so that the vehicles could drive off.

They were soon on the move once more. They left the boat behind and drove along the jetty. They kept passing red signs in French.

'What do they mean?' asked Nicholas. All at once a huge French truck came thundering straight at them, horn blaring and lights flashing.

'Drive on the other side of the road!' Mrs King

yelled and her husband swerved wildly.

'Phew! That's what those signs meant. I forgot the French drive on the right.'

Going rather slowly they managed to reach the centre of the old French town without being hooted at too often. They found a place to park and then took to their feet, feeling much safer that way. They began to enjoy themselves at last. It was really fun. All the shops were the same as English ones, but different. You could go to the baker but it wasn't called that and it sold different types of bread. The butcher looked the same at first, but then they noticed the meat was different somehow.

Eventually they found a little restaurant where they decided to have lunch. Mrs King picked up the menu and stared at it. 'I can't understand it,' she said. 'It's all in French.' At last a waiter came over and spoke quickly. He was obviously waiting for an order. Mr King looked at him in alarm, wondering how he could even begin to explain.

But the waiter smiled and nodded.

'Ah – English?' he asked.

'Yes!' said Mr King, with great relief.

'I will read you the menu,' said the waiter, and bit by bit he went through the different dishes, while the Kings licked their lips, or pulled horrible faces.

'And this is Frog's Legs In Sauce,' he said. 'And this is tiny – how do you say – sheeps?'

'Tiny sheep?' murmured Mrs King. 'Do you mean lambs? Baaa baaa?'

'No no!' laughed the waiter. 'I mean how you say – shreeps? Sheemps?'

'Shrimps!' Lucy shouted suddenly. 'He means shrimps!'

'Yes, yes, shreemps,' went on the waiter.

'I'm sorry we can't speak any French,' Mrs King said.

'Doesn't matter, doesn't matter.' The waiter wrote down their order.

Mr King leaned across the table and whispered at Lucy. 'Do you really want snails in garlic butter? It sounds revolting. Remember that we have to go back on the boat soon. We don't want you being sick all over the place.'

'I like snails,' said Lucy.

'You've never had them!'

'But I do like them.'

When the snails arrived Lucy was not so certain. Seven big shells sat on her plate. They looked as if they were about to get up and slide off at any moment. The others sat and watched her. They had chosen simple things like chicken or 'shreemps'.

Lucy poked one of the snails gingerly with her fork. It toppled over. She looked at her mother. 'How do you get it out?' she whispered.

'Here snail! Here boy!' coaxed Nicholas,

bending over a shell.

'Stop it at once,' snapped their mother. 'Try using your fork, Lucy.'

Lucy held the shell with one hand and tried to lever her fork inside. She struggled for ages, twisting her fork every way until suddenly the snail shot out of the shell, whizzed right across the restaurant and hit the window. There it stuck, slowly slipping down further and further, leaving a trail of garlic butter. Lucy pretended that nothing had happened, even though half the restaurant was now staring in her direction.

'Lucy!' hissed her mother.

'I couldn't help it. It wouldn't come out.' She tried again on a second snail, but that was just as difficult. This time the whole snail, shell and all, shot across the table and got Mr King on the chest.

'Thank you,' he said stonily. 'If I had wanted snails I would have ordered them.' He wiped his greasy shirt with a napkin.

Lucy decided she needed a bit of extra help. She glared hard at a snail shell on her plate, feeling the power gathering in her eyes. She was getting good at controlling it by now and knew just how much force to put into her startling fireball gaze. The shell began to sizzle and crack, then it fell away from the meat inside. Lucy heaved a sigh, stuck her fork in and ate the snail in its sauce of garlic butter. The others watched as she chewed, rolling the food round her cheeks. Lucy closed her eyes.

'It's delicious!' she murmured. 'Utterly delicious!' She opened her eyes and pushed a shell over to her father. 'You try. They're gorgeous!'

'Er, no thank you Lucy. Not this time. I'm full,' said Mr King lamely.

'I'll try,' said her mother.

So Lucy concentrated her gaze again and split open another shell, handing over the meat to Mrs King.

'I must say, they're not at all bad,' agreed Mrs King a moment later.

Lucy managed to get all the shells open the same way. Several people stared at her very hard, but they couldn't quite believe it. They told themselves there wasn't really a girl smashing up snail shells with her eyebeams. By the time the Kings left, the whole restaurant was talking about the mystery. Whatever would Lightning Lucy do next?

8

A Case of Mistaken Identity

'We really must go to the hypermarket before we get the ferry back,' said Mr King.

Mrs King was sitting on a low wall, looking out over the harbour.

'What do we want to go there for?' she asked. 'Can't we stay here? My feet are getting tired of all this wandering about.'

'Do you want a lift, Mum?' asked Lucy, with a sly grin.

'No thanks Lucy. I know just what your *lifts* are like. Before I know it I shall be doing a triple loop and breaking the sound barrier.'

Mr King shuffled his feet impatiently. 'Come on. We've got to catch the ferry in an hour. We haven't much time to collect our duty free allowance.'

'So that's what all the hurry is about,' cried Mrs King. 'You just want to make sure you have plenty of wine to take back. Typical. Come on then, we'd better get going.'

On the way Mr King explained to Lucy and Nicholas what the duty free allowance was. 'When you take some things into Britain from another country you have to pay tax on them, because they are much cheaper over here than they are in Britain.'

'What sort of things?' asked Nicholas.

'Wine, perfume, watches, things like that. But, when you're abroad, like we are now, you are allowed to take back a little for yourself without paying the tax, and that's called . . .'

'Duty free allowance,' finished Lucy.

In the hypermarket the Kings found a whole wall stacked from top to bottom with wine bottles. There were massive crates of beer standing on the floor. People were pulling out crate after crate and throwing them into their trolleys. It was a madhouse, and Dad joined in with a wild grin.

Mrs King looked at the growing pile of wine and beer. 'Is that enough?' she asked at last, a trifle stiffly.

'Just a couple more,' said Dad.

'Don't go over the duty-free limit, will you?' warned Mrs King.

Mr King turned a shade red as he put two more bottles in the trolley. 'One or two extra won't hurt,' he said. 'The Customs officers won't worry about that.'

'Dad!' shouted Lucy. 'Suppose you're arrested?'

'They won't arrest me for two bottles. If they

find them I shall just have to pay the duty on them. That's all.'

Mrs King groaned. 'I smell trouble,' she said.

They caught the ferry with a little time to spare and at last they were able to rest after their long day in Boulogne. Lucy and Nicholas rested for at least three minutes before they went dashing off to see where the front of the ship was, and then where the back of the ship was. Then they went to see what was on one side and then on the other. They explored upstairs, downstairs and were back after twenty minutes, by which time Mr and Mrs King were snoozing in their recliner seats.

The ship's siren woke them as they entered harbour. Passengers were already streaming down stairs to the car decks to get back in their vehicles. Mr King hustled Nicholas and Lucy into the back seat and pushed a rug at his daughter. 'Cover that box with the wine in it, Lucy. With a bit of luck the Customs men will never notice.'

Engines started and cars began to roll off the ferry on to the dock. They came to a large sign which said NOTHING TO DECLARE and pointed to the left. Mr King followed the arrow.

'I hope you know what you're doing,' muttered Mrs King anxiously.

'Of course I do. I've only got six extra bottles.'

'Six! I thought you said it was a couple!' Mrs King stared at her husband with eyes like a dragon.

'Yes, well, I made a slight mistake in my adding up...' he began.

'Oooh! You ought to be shot!'

'Dad – suppose you get caught?' wailed Nicholas.

'I won't. Look, for heaven's sake, it's only a little extra and I can pay the extra duty.'

At that moment they came to the Customs shed. The cars drove into different lanes and Customs officers took a quick look at each one and waved them on. Mr King drove up with a cheerful smile. A Customs officer stepped forward and halted the car.

'Anything to declare Sir?'

'No – we've just got the usual wine and beer. That's all.'

The officer peered into the depths of the car. He nodded at Lucy and Nicholas. 'These your children Sir?'

Mr King could not help himself. 'No. I bought them at the hypermarket.'

The officer stared at Mr King icily. 'Very funny Sir. Would you pull your car over there so we can inspect your luggage please?' And he pointed to where a line of cars were having everything taken out for inspection.

Mr King drove over to the line.

'You stupid idiot!' hissed Mrs King. 'You and your big mouth. You had to be clever-clever didn't you? Now you'll have to own up about the extra wine and it serves you right.'

The Kings had to get out of the car and a Customs officer stood over them and told them what to unpack. Out came the bags and everything in the bags, out came seats, out came anything that could be taken out, including the case with the rug over the top.

Lucy stared at the case and watched the officer. She had the beginnings of an idea that could just help Dad out of his trouble. Mrs King was busy in the front of the car. Mr King was opening the bonnet. The Customs officer was leaning over the engine.

Lucy's hair began to crackle faintly, little sparks jerked and juddered from her finger-tips and the wine case lifted from the ground. Her simple idea was to get it up in the air, out of sight until the inspection was over. Gradually the wine case rose higher and higher, above everyone's head. Lucy smiled. This was easy-peasy!

'Hey! Hey! That's our wine up there!' Suddenly Lucy was thrown to one side as several people came thundering past. They climbed up the King's car and tried to get at the flying wine case. Instinctively Lucy made it fly away from them, and a desperate chase began. Others began to shout and join in. People clambered on to car roofs and stampeded across bonnets. They leaped on to other cars and tried to stand on people's shoulders.

Lucy tried to control the crazy case of wine that everybody thought belonged to them, but she was rapidly disappearing in a heaving, shouting mob of travellers. Several people started to climb the iron pillars to the roof. They swung from girders like a troup of baboons as they tried to get their hands on the flying case.

'Oi! That's our case of wine up there!'

'No it isn't? Get your hands off!'

'Hey, stop shoving, you fat twit!'

'Who are you calling a fat twit? Take that!'

The Customs shed was now a mass of wriggling, wrestling, screaming, yelling people. The wine case flew about in uncontrollable loops and dives as Lucy was shoved one way, then another. Whistles blew, sirens wailed and at last there was an almighty crash as the wine case dive-bombed a truck carrying more wine from France. Bottles

shattered all over the place and wine poured like Niagara Falls across the concrete floor of the shed.

At once the shouts died away. Everybody stood still. They stared at the growing lake of wine and they sniffed. What a pong! Like a million florist shops! Several Customs officers ran to the truck.

'This isn't wine,' one cried. 'It's perfume. It's a truck-load of perfume in wine bottles. Somebody's trying to smuggle perfume through in wine bottles!'

Lightning Lucy scrambled to her feet and gave her electric hair a little shake. She was just in time to see the truck owners being arrested, and everybody else go back to their cars.

'Did you see that? asked Nicholas excitedly. 'They caught some real smugglers!'

'It was the flying wine case that interested me,' said Mrs King, staring very hard at her daughter.

They were interrupted by a Customs man. 'Okay, you can pack your car now and go.'

'Go?' said Mr King in disbelief.

'Oh yes. We've done our work for today. We've been after that perfume smuggling gang for months. We knew they were getting it into this country to sell cheaply, but we didn't know how. Well, we've got them now.'

Lucy sighed with relief. The Customs officers were so pleased with themselves they had forgotten to ask how the trouble had begun.

Mr King packed up the car and drove away. 'Boy,' he began. 'That was a lucky escape. I thought we were done for.' He gave a smile and started to laugh. 'Six extra bottles of wine!'

'You should be ashamed of yourself,' said Mrs King.

Lucy tapped her father on the shoulder. 'Er, Dad, I'm afraid there's one problem. You see, that case of wine that was flying about, well...'

The car screeched to a halt. Dad was as white as a soggy meringue. 'No! It wasn't! But that was ALL my wine! ALL of it! TWELVE bottles!'

'I was trying to help. It seemed like such a simple idea – so easy.'

'So simple it nearly caused a riot.' said Mrs King.

'Twelve bottles,' groaned Dad.

'Poetic justice. It serves you right for trying to cheat,' said Mrs King.

Nicholas was gazing at his big sister. 'You've caught a gang of smugglers,' he said. 'Wow!'

At this, Lucy perked up a bit. She even got a bit big-headed. 'So I have! I caught the perfume smuggling gang... wow!'

Mr King held his head in his hands and moaned.

'Twelve bottles of wine, all gone. Oh wow.'